MathStart®
SEQUENCING

Rabbit's Pajama Party

BY **STUART J. MURPHY**

ILLUSTRATED BY

FRANK REMKIEWICZ

HarperCollins*Publishers*

LEVEL
1

To Maureen and Randy and all the pajama parties in their future

—S.J.M.

For Kate and Sarah, who teach in sequence

—F.R.

The illustrations in this book were done in watercolor and Prismacolors on Bristol paper.

HarperCollins®, 🖋®, and MathStart® are trademarks of HarperCollins Publishers Inc.
For more information about the MathStart Series, please write to HarperCollins
Children's Books, 10 East 53rd Street, New York, NY 10022, or visit our web site at
http://www.harperchildrens.com.

Bugs incorporated in the MathStart series design were painted by Jon Buller.

Rabbit's Pajama Party
Text copyright © 1999 by Stuart J. Murphy
Illustrations copyright © 1999 by Frank Remkiewicz
Printed in the U.S.A. All rights reserved.

Library of Congress Cataloging-in-Publication Data
Murphy, Stuart J., date
 Rabbit's pajama party / by Stuart J. Murphy ; illustrated by Frank Remkiewicz.
   p.   cm. — (MathStart)
 "Level 1, sequencing."
 Summary: A group of animal friends have fun at a pajama party
while demonstrating activities that happen in a particular order
or sequence.
 ISBN 0-06-027616-9. — ISBN 0-06-027617-7 (lib. bdg.).
 ISBN 0-06-446722-8 (pbk.)
 1. Sequences (Mathematics)—Juvenile literature.
[1. Sequences (Mathematics)] I. Remkiewicz, Frank, ill.
II. Title.   III. Series.
QA292.M87 1999   98-36617
515'.24—dc21   CIP
                                          AC

Typography by Michele N. Tupper
1 2 3 4 5 6 7 8 9 10
❖
First Edition

Rabbit's Pajama Party

My pajama party is about to begin!

I run to the door and let my friends in.

We gobble our dinner,
pizza with cheese,

9

and slurp down our fruit juice,
as much as we please.

For dessert we make sundaes,
hot fudge and whipped cream,

with a cherry on top—
an elephant's dream.

14

o we pull on our pj's—
mine are bright red.

Then Mom says,
"It's time to get ready for bed."

"Now into your sleeping bags.
Zip them up tight."

When everyone's ready,
Mom says, "All right!"

19

Elephant giggles,
and I start to laugh!

Mom takes one last picture.
"Good night!" shouts Giraffe.

But the fun has just started.
We don't want to rest.

29

We tell scary stories—
the kind we like best.

There's a "Boo,"
then a scream
and a "Shhhh,"
then a roar.

But after a while
all I hear
is Mouse snore.

letting friends in

eating dinner

making sundaes

putting on PJ's

getting into sleeping bags

saying good night

What Happened at Rabbit's Pajama Party

FOR ADULTS AND KIDS

In *Rabbit's Pajama Party*, the math concept presented is time sequencing. Understanding what comes first, what comes next, what happens after that, and what happens last is important in the development of a child's understanding of mathematics as well as story comprehension.

If you would like to have more fun with the math concepts presented in *Rabbit's Pajama Party*, here are a few suggestions:

• Read the story with the child and describe what is going on in each picture. Ask, "What do you think will happen next?"

• While reading the story, point out the sequence of events in the pictures. Encourage the child to tell the story using the words "first," "next," "then," and "last."

• After reading the story, ask, "What happened first?" "What happened next?" "Then what happened?" "What was the last thing that happened?"

• Make a timeline for the story. For example, at 5:00 the friends arrive, at 6:00 they eat pizza, and so on.

• Together, discuss events that require steps in a particular order or sequence—for example, making a peanut-butter-and-jelly sandwich. Write down the steps as the child dictates them and then make the sandwich, following the steps exactly. If they are not in the correct sequence, discuss what went wrong and make corrections.